ABSOLU TERRIFIED

Copyright © 2021

ISBN: 9798478887230

'Absolutely Terrified'

Author Moray L.W.H. McGuffie

Cover design by Moray L.W.H. McGuffie

Book design by Moray L.W.H. McGuffie

Cover image by Jan Baars from Pixabay

First Book Printing: 2021

ABSOLUTELY TERRIFIED

The hilarious true story of a first-time flight in a light aircraft

By Moray LWH McGuffie

Author of A Fall From The Top

CHAPTERS...

ACKNOWLEDGEMENTS...

To my wonderful wife Desiree and my fantastic children, who are now all grown up. Hannah, Megan, Matthew, Bethan, Samuel & Elena.

I would also like to say a big thank you to Craig Rees for writing the foreword to this book.

A TRUE STORY...

I have shared the details of this terrifying true story on many occasions over the years with individuals, as well as larger audiences. Recounting the horrifying tale at a wide range of events and business functions in the UK and overseas.

It feels as if I was in a film when I think back and remember the day, because of the vivid memories I still have. As unbelievable as the story may sound, it really happened in the way that I describe it. Some of the technical information I provide may not be entirely correct. Although, I do believe they will give you a good idea of my experiences.

First, I would like to give enormous thanks to the pilot, whose name I no longer remember.

He made a sterling effort in flying the plane as safely as possible, in what were incredibly hard conditions.

No doubt, the pilot had experienced difficult weather conditions many times before this eventful occurrence. Whereas in my case, until this particular day, I had only been through a few bumpy flights on much larger passenger aircraft.

I am more than delighted to say that I am still alive to tell the incredible tale.

Hopefully, you can have a good chuckle at my expense.

I must admit that I laughed a few times myself as I wrote about the terrifying emotions that I went through.

FORWARD...

Ps. Craig Rees

Moray is a gifted storyteller, who has a talent for blending humour and his own personal experiences into tales that will take you on a rollercoaster of emotions, but always leave you crying with laughter at the end.

I have had the privilege of hearing many of Moray's stories which are all based on his varied and unbelievable life. But by far the infamous aeroplane story is my favourite. I can recall the very first time I heard it as the whole audience lived through every nail-biting moment as the drama unfolded.

There were gasps at near death moments and screams of laughter at situations that you would not have thought possible.

My only sadness was that the experience was over too soon as I wanted to hear it again. Thanks to this book I can!

I am so glad Moray has taken the time to write this story as some tales need telling more than once. So can I encourage you to fasten your seatbelts and join Moray for the ride of your life... And be prepared to use the emergency exits if you find yourself laughing a bit too hard.

BASIC FLYING RULES...

One:

Try to stay in the middle of the air

Two:

Do not go near the edges of it.

Three:

The edges of the air can be recognised by the appearance of the ground, buildings, sea, trees, and interstellar space. It is much more difficult to fly there.

Anonymous

TERRIFIED...

Definition:

VERY FRIGHTENED

Synonyms:

HORROR-STRUCK

PETRIFIED

HORRIFIED

†

WHY DON'T YOU CHARTER A PLANE?

Chapter One – Making plans for an exciting day

I have shared this horrific experience, for your amusement. The images of the event have been indelibly etched into my memory. Thinking about it still makes me shudder to this day. It is quite simply something that I will never forget.

That is a fact!

This truly horrific event occurred around the year of 1992.

I was in my early 30s and probably at the peak of my career. My immediate boss had recently awarded me the nickname, "Quantum Leap", because I had climbed the promotion ladder so quickly.

In a one-to-one meeting, he set me on a targeted programme that he estimated would take seven years to achieve. Through very hard work and much effort, as well as making many sacrifices, I reached his target in just a two-year period. I must admit, I was very proud of the fact.

From a standing start, I had built a very successful network of sales offices. They stretched across Wales and part of the Southwest of England.

The operation was comprised of a team of well over 250 self-employed, commission only advisors and managers.

They met with the public and business owners, advising on various life assurance, investment, and pension products

The bulk of my income was generated by taking an override commission percentage on every product that was sold. My pay checks were substantial, and were increasing exponentially.

At the time, I was earning more money than I had ever dreamed of. Along with that, I led the lifestyle that I believed went along with it. I wore expensive handmade Savile Row suits made by my personal tailor, along with silk ties and brightly coloured handkerchiefs carefully placed into my breast pocket. I felt like a million dollars.

I lived in a beautiful country village in a large, new executive house in an expensive area. On the drive outside of the property, I had a range of six high-priced, high-performance sports and large saloon cars. I had a routine that meant I drove in a different one each day of the week. On some days, I literally had to pinch myself.

I genuinely thought that I had made it. I had made plans with my bosses to retire at 40, as a multi-millionaire. The future certainly looked bright at the time. A couple of years later, things would transform dramatically. That, however, is another story altogether.

Hence the reason that I could afford to charter a private plane to take me to what was going to be a very important business meeting.

My business connections had presented me with an amazing opportunity to take over another region of salespeople, managers, and offices. The outcome of successful negotiations would mean that I would be able to merge the additional territory with my own region. The result of this would increase the size of my group by almost one third. Added to this, the exciting news was that it would add a sizeable amount of money to my income, pushing me even closer to the goals I had set myself.

When I heard the news of the opportunity. I acted quickly, planning to meet the managers and sales teams from the region at a hotel in Exeter, the capital city of Devon, the very next day.

This would have meant leaving Swansea incredibly early in the morning, which was not normally a problem because I drove long distances most days.

I knew, however, that there were currently endless stretches of heavy road works on the motorway, which were causing some long delays. I knew from experience, having been held up myself in the traffic a few times.

Added to that, I also had previously organised an important recruitment seminar that I couldn't rearrange at short notice for the same day at 7 pm in the evening at a Swansea hotel. I didn't want to spend a lot of time sat in my car being unproductive. I was stuck between a rock and a hard place.

I met with my excellent Personal Assistant Sue in my Swansea open plan office that overlooked the city. We discussed the problem in detail, doing our very best to come up with a viable solution. Considering the driving time, as well as the likely delays, making a couple of presentation and holding several meetings.

There simply were not enough hours in the day to make it workable. I was feeling quite frustrated.

We were both sat in my office, having considered every possibility we could think of. When suddenly, Sue's eyes lit up and she said, "Why don't you charter a private plane from Swansea airport"?

"That's a great idea. But how much will that cost me"? I asked. "I haven't got a clue," she replied. "I will make some calls to find out".

She quickly stood up from her chair, dutifully leaving my office, and went off to make some telephone call enquiries. First, to find out whether chartering a private plane was indeed possible, and of course, the price of the flight, which I expected to be quite expensive.

At the time, I had only been living mid-week in an apartment that I had recently purchased in a modern new development on the Swansea Marina. I had only visited the shops and restaurants.

I had never heard of, or for that matter, even been near to the local airport as far as I was aware.

When Sue mentioned the name of it, I naturally assumed that it was just another regional site.

Similar to others in the UK, operating commercial flights that fly excited holiday makers to destinations such as Spain, Portugal, and other sunny places throughout Europe.

In fact, my assumption could not have been further from the truth. I would soon discover that the only thing that the airport had in common with hubs like Birmingham, Manchester, and Cardiff was that it was actually called an 'airport'. All other similarities ended right there.

After a short while, Sue came into my office with a huge grin on her face and said, "I have some good news. I have managed to charter you a private plane that will leave Swansea airport at 7 am tomorrow and bring you back at 4.30 pm.

The flight will take around 45 minutes". "That's Brilliant Sue"! I replied, "How much will it cost"?

To my complete amazement, the flight from Swansea to Exeter, plus the return flight in a private aircraft, was only going to be a cost of £250 all in. I couldn't believe the price.

I had honestly been expecting to be quoted a much higher cost than that. "A real bargain", I thought to myself. I was so chuffed and excited that I didn't think for a moment to consider what type of aircraft that I would actually be flying in to get me to Exeter. I would find out pretty soon.

Sue handed me a phone number on a slip of paper and said, "Because it is short notice, you need to call them right away to confirm all the arrangements". I thanked her for doing such a great job, and asked her, "By the way Sue, can you tell me the name of the airline that I will fly with"?

She hesitated for a moment and said, "Oh, it's called Air Aid", she replied with a big smile.

"Sorry, what did you say. Air Raid!", I exclaimed, feeling quite concerned.

In fits of laughter, she slowly explained,". "No Moray, the name is AIR.....AID", carefully pronouncing each word along with a clear gap between them twice to make sure that I completely understood.

"Thanks Sue. Got it. That's a weird name", I replied slightly nervously. At that moment, I questioned whether I was really making the right decision.

I thought about the name for a few seconds. I picked up the telephone handset and punched in the number. The telephone made the ringing sound once. I was greeted by a cheerful man who answered and said, "Good morning, this is Air Aid Swansea". I replied, "Hi, this is Moray McGuffie speaking. I am calling to confirm a private flight booking to and from Exeter for tomorrow".

"That's right Mr McGuffie, can you meet me at the airport at 6.45 am? "Yes, of course, I will meet you tomorrow", "Smashing", he replied enthusiastically. "That's terrific", I answered.

"Oh, just one more thing before you go. Can you tell me where I can find you in the passenger terminal"?

There was a brief and awkward pause on the line, which was quickly followed by a surprised chuckle. He replied, "Er, sorry, there is no passenger terminal here mate. It's not a problem. You will see our hut from the road on the left as you drive into the airport. You can't miss it. You have got our name, haven't you? It's Air...Aid, OK? I will see you in the morning". He gave a clear pronunciation of the two words in exactly the way that Sue had done.

No doubt other people had experienced the same misunderstanding, likening the company name to some kind of bombing mission.

I could hear some amusement in his voice as he spoke. "OK thank you, I will see you tomorrow morning at 6.45 am", I said rather nervously, questioning my sanity.

As we said our goodbye's, I imagined him sharing the amusing story with some of his flying pals. Telling them about the business executive who had asked to meet him in the non-existent Swansea passenger terminal. He must have thought to himself, "What an idiot".

I would have thought the same in his position. I certainly would have told the tale to get a laugh from my friends.

I have to admit, that at this point, I felt rather foolish and embarrassed.

I was glad that no one was in my office to hear the conversation at the time.

As I put the phone down in its cradle, I asked myself if I had gone crazy, thinking, "Are you really sure that you know what you are doing"? To be certain, the next day was going to be a very eventful one, to say the least.

At this point, I realised that I was getting more than a little anxious. These feelings would change on the next morning.

They would, in fact, get much worse. If I knew what was going to happen, I would have taken my chances on the motorway.

HORRIFIED...

Definition:

VERY SHOCKED

Synonyms:

AGHAST

AFRAID

TROUBLED

WHAT ON EARTH HAVE I GONE AND DONE?

Chapter Two – Gosh, it really is very windy today

I got up nice and early the next morning to hear the sound of very strong winds buffeting on the windows of my marina apartment. I looked out of the window to see very heavy dark rain clouds that filled the sky. It appeared as if it was really blowing a gale outside.

I reasoned with myself, "The wind is always much worse when you live near to the sea. It's probably not going to be too bad".

When I left my apartment. I quickly realised that the wind was far worse than I had previously imagined. In fact, it was so bad that I had to lean forward at an angle and forcefully push myself through it as I made my way to my car.

When I opened the door, I needed to tightly grip the handle to stop it from being blown out of my hand. It really was blowing a gale. I thought, "I hope it calms down by the time I get to the airport".

The drive from the Marina to the airport was very scenic after I got out of the town centre.

The Welsh countryside and village properties that I drove past on my journey pleasantly surprised me.

As I travelled, the more I could feel very heavy gusts of wind pushing harder and harder against my car. I had to take extra care to control the steering wheel.

Conditions steadily grew worse the closer I got to my destination. The weather was really quite bad indeed, while the trees on the roads were bending under the force of the high winds.

The sky was continuing to get even darker. I wondered whether the gale was, in fact, going to be a storm. The further I drove, the more uneasy I felt about my flight.

It really surprised me when I finally reached Swansea airport. It certainly wasn't what I had been expecting in any way at all. In fact, it was really just an old airfield that was in an exceptionally barren part of the area. It was very exposed to the conditions, because it was quite close to the well-known picturesque Gower coastline.

Just as was explained on the previous day, there was no passenger terminal, or anything at all like it. All I could see from my car was a control tower, some ramshackle old buildings, and wooden sheds.

Other than that, there were a few small two-seater aircraft that were standing on tarmac or grass, dotted about here and there. It felt as if I was in the middle of nowhere.

As I arrived, just as the man on the telephone had said I would, I saw the Air Aid hut straight away.

"Good", I thought. However, the sight of what was standing next to it honestly filled me with great fear. It looked as if it was the aircraft that I was going to fly in. "Oh, no"! I exclaimed as I made my turn into the airport.

I think it is important to clarify something at this point of the story.

I use the term "aircraft" as a very loose description of what I observed. At first sight, I could only describe it as a small three-wheeled car that looked a little like the fibreglass Reliant Robins that used to be on the roads when I was young. It had a propeller attached to the front end of it.

To be honest, it appeared to be quite flimsy and didn't look as if it was in any way safe to fly in, to me. My confidence levels sunk.

It had wings that appeared as if someone had either glued or screwed them onto its roof. These were strengthened by connecting bars that went from the underside of the wings into the bodywork.

What frightened me even more though, was the fact that the rickety looking little Reliant Robin type aircrafts were being violently. They jerked around and wobbled back and forth by the force of the strong winds.

So much so, that it looked as if it would be blown upside down at any given moment! "What on earth have I done"? I asked myself.

I parked my car and opened the door. I sat there for a few moments, once again questioning my sanity. The winds were much stronger than they were at the Marina. As before, I had to lean my body forwards into the strong winds as I walked towards the aircraft hut.

At this point, I wondered whether the very inclement weather was, in fact, a hurricane. Well, it certainly felt like one to me.

As I got closer to the air hut, I noticed that one-half of the engine bonnet of the aircraft was lifted up. After taking a couple more paces, I discovered a man who was bent over into the compartment who appeared to be working on the engine.

From the little I could see, I determined that he was checking the engine oil. He was bending over so far into the compartment that I could not see his face. He appeared to be shabbily dressed, which concerned me a little. The man was wearing a thick grey woolly jumper that was quite tatty, along with an old pair of jogging bottoms. His position meant that I could only see his back and legs. It appeared as if he was to lean over just a couple of more inches. He would have fallen right into the hole.

The weather was so bad that I had to shout at the top of my voice, "Hi, I am Moray McGuffie. I am here for my flight"!

He didn't move at all, but shouted back to me in a very muffled voice, "Oh, good morning Sir".

He paused for a moment, and shouted, "Tell you what. Wait inside the hut for me out of the wind. I am just making some safety checks. I will be with you shortly".

"Great", I replied, and pushed into the wind once again, until I made it through the door. I was grateful to get out of the cold.

I entered what was really an enormous garden shed with some old office furniture inside. It was quite untidy at first sight. The best way I can describe it is that it was as if I had stepped back in time to the World War two era.

As I waited, I looked out of the window and watched the plane's wings go up and down sharply in the strong winds. It appeared as if the man working on the aircraft was actually using his weight to keep it on the ground.

The weather was indeed terrible. After a few minutes, he stood up straight, pulled the bonnet down and turned towards me.

What I saw next, both shocked and horrified me even more. The man had white hair that was Brylcreemed back over his head. He was also quite overweight, appearing to be aged about seventy or more years to start with.

As he moved towards the Hut, I immediately noticed that his left arm and hand were very awkwardly contorted in what appeared to be a disabled fashion held closely to his chest. He resembled a person who had survived a serious stroke. Worse than that, as he walked towards me, he dragged his left leg along the ground behind him, rather like a zombie from an old black and white horror movie.

I couldn't believe what I was watching. I remember standing there with my mouth wide open in amazement, thinking, "Oh no. Is he the pilot who is going to be flying me to Exeter"?.

I am certain that there is no other way to describe the way I was feeling as I watched him struggle to walk past the window. I was completely and utterly flabbergasted!

He awkwardly made his way into the hut, having to pause for a moment so he could lift his good leg over the threshold of the door. As he entered, He cheerfully said, "Morning Sir". He looked upwards and inelegantly reached up to the roof joists and tugged on a red cord that hung down, until eventually, after some effort, a bright yellow life jacket fell onto the floor by his feet.

He promptly picked it up off the floor, tossed it to me and said, "Right Sir, you will need to put that on". I caught it and looked at it for a couple of seconds. I asked somewhat nervously, "Why do I need this"?, feeling more frightened than ever.

"Well, to get to Exeter, you will be flying over water you see", he replied.

He spoke to me in the way a parent would explain something important or complicated to a very young child. I realised that he had worked out that I was feeling quite ill at ease.

I must have gone white with fear. "Of course. How stupid am I"? I thought to myself. His answer to my question made complete sense.

I had not considered that flying over the sea was the quickest route. For some reason, I thought the flight

would be along the coast- line or where you could see the motorway, which would have meant a much longer journey in either case.

I stood there feeling quite naïve, thinking that things were going from what was terrible, too much worse. Now, I was even more terrified, if that was even possible.

What he went on to say didn't reassure me, "If the plane goes down in the sea, you will need it, won't you". "Oh cheers, that is really great news, ", I thought sarcastically.

My silent sarcasm continued on, "Thanks very much mate, I really wanted to hear those encouraging words. Thanks for reassuring me. I definitely feel a lot better now"!

The irony of the situation was that I often used jokes about flying as a warmup for attendees when I spoke at meetings or ran training courses. I had a range of complete routines, with many of the gags in my repertoire involving being frightened of flying. They did not seem so funny as I stood there.

He watched me in the way an examiner would. Carefully scrutinising my technique as I nervously placed the life jacket over my head, remembering to tie the surrounding cords in the same way that air hostesses do when they explain the important steps passengers must take in emergency situations. For the next few minutes, we chatted about flying in general.

While we were in conversation, out of the corner of my peripheral vision, I could still see the plane rocking backwards and forwards in the very strong winds. As they blew against the hut, they found small gaps in the joints, making high-pitched whistling sounds that filled the air.

Seeing the plane being shaken so much outside made me feel even more anxious. I questioned whether the elderly chap could even control the plane at his age in the awful weather conditions, especially with what appeared to be just one good functioning arm.

I was just about to ask when we would leave, as a man pulled up in a car outside of the hut. He appeared to be about the same age as me. He briskly came into the hut and said, introducing himself, "Hi, you must be Moray, I am your pilot".

Phew! The incredible sense of relief I felt at that moment was immense. I truly was delighted to meet him. As I stood there, I made sure that I controlled my emotions, remaining outwardly calm as we shook hands. Inside though, I was joyfully jumping up and down clicking my heels together, raising my hands in the air shouting "WEHEY...YES...WOHOO...HOORAY...WHAT A RESULT"!

I am certain that the feelings of euphoria that I experienced at that time were exactly the same as if I had just scored the winning goal in the FA Cup Final at Wembley stadium in the last minute of extra time. I remained silently elated.

"Goodness me," I thought, or words to that effect, I certainly felt a lot better.

Using entirely the wrong analogy for the situation. Surely, it would mean smooth sailing now.

Wouldn't it?

PETRIFIED...

Definition:

EXTREMELY NERVOUS

Synonyms:

TERROR STRUCK

STUNNED

BENUMBED

PLEASE GOD. DON'T LET ME DIE!

Chapter Three – An all but brief moment of relief

My incredible feelings of genuine relief very sadly turned out to be very short-lived indeed. This was because as soon as I climbed into the cockpit of the aircraft to take my seat, I quickly became extremely anxious again.

First of all, the aircraft was still being violently rocked from side to side by the heavy winds, even though we were in a stationary position.

Secondly, the engine would not start immediately, which reminded me of the times in my younger days, when I had tried starting some of my old clapped-out cars.

I remembered myself being sat in my car driver's seat, twisting the ignition key, turning the engine repeatedly, hoping and praying that it would eventually catch and start. This seemed to be no different from those memories at all. I remember thinking as I watched the pilot, "You couldn't make this up".

When he eventually managed to get the engine going, the noise was almost deafening.

This once again took me back to the Second World War. Reminding me of the old spitfires and hurricanes that I saw in black and white war movies when I was a child.

The pilot handed me a black pair of headphones with a microphone attached to the headset, gesturing that I should put them on. As I placed them on my head, I looked around the cockpit, which genuinely seemed as if it really was out of a war movie. It didn't look like anything modern.

I put my safety belt on and noticed that we were sitting awfully close together on what appeared to be bench seats that had cheap foam and plastic stuck to them. My confidence levels at this point were now even lower, to say the very least.

The pilot cheerfully stuck both of his thumbs up to me and shouted, "Okay. Let's go"!

He then radioed the control tower. From memory, this is the way the conversation went:

Pilot: "Good morning tower. This is R9546, (I can't remember the actual number) requesting permission to proceed to runway one. Over".

Control Tower: " Good morning R9546. Recommend that you don't use runway one. The wind is so bad that you probably will not get off the ground. Please proceed to runway two. Over".

Pilot: Thanks for that tower. I wondered when I saw the weather this morning. I was quite concerned about the wind. Proceeding as instructed to runway two. Over"

I honestly could not believe what I heard on my headphones. I really was scared now. I must admit that I wondered if I was on Candid Camera for a few moments.

As we taxied slowly towards the runway, it felt as if the plane was going to start falling apart because of the way the wind was banging and rocking us from side to side.

Finally, we reached the end of the runway as instructed and waited patiently as we continued to be shaken. The clearance came to take off. The pilot revved the engine until it was almost screaming. He let off the brake, and we lurched forward with a jump, bumping up the runway as if we were driving along a cobbled road.

I could still hear the sound of the wind well above the engine noise as it bashed against the plane. We hurtled along for some time until, after what seemed ages, we took off.

As we did, the pilot looked at me while loudly saying with an enormous grin, "Ha ha ha! You certainly picked a fine day for your first flight in a light aircraft". I smiled nervously and looked out of my passenger window, expecting to see a view of the airport.

Instead, I just saw the wing of the aircraft and grass. A tremendous gust of wind had blown us onto our side at a 45-degree angle. It seemed as if the ground was just a few feet away from the wing tip.

I held on to the bottom of my seat for dear life. I was no longer terrified or horrified. I was in fact petrified.

The pilot yelled "Whoa"! as he wrestled with the steering control to get us flying straight again. I can say that at the time, I didn't believe in God.

In fact, I considered myself to be an atheist. In those few seconds, my atheistic beliefs disappeared, because I can honestly tell you I quietly prayed as I tightly gripped the frame under my seat, hanging on for dear life.

I had once considered myself to be quite a hard man. I had been a long-time practitioner and professional karate instructor. I had endured many beatings from my own instructors over the years. I had learned how to deal with things like fear.

Added to that, I also believed that I was a dynamic, ruthless, hard-nosed business executive that was not what you would call a softy. My prayer at that moment was audibly silent, but in my head, I was loudly screaming and tearfully begging, "Please God, don't let me die"!

The engine laboured quite a lot as we climbed towards the clouds. The plane was constantly being violently shaken and buffeted by the powerful winds.

We eventually flew into the clouds to meet with what looked like thick fog, along with heavy rain that suddenly appeared from nowhere, harshly hitting the windshield. The pilot reached out his right arm and turned on the windscreen wipers.

As they moved, they screeched from side to side and were not in any way effective. All we could see in front of us were dark grey clouds, which were so thick that we could not even see past the propeller which created a dark circle just a few feet in front of us. It was terrifying.

In addition, it seemed as if we were trying our best to fly in a straight line, but we were constantly being thrown from side to side as well as up and down by the winds. For all I knew, we could have been flying in any direction.

Every time the wind hit the aircraft; it created a loud bang. The only way I can describe it would be to say that it felt just like being in a bumper car at the funfair, when you are hit at full speed in a head on collision.

There was a big difference though, as this was happening about every five seconds.

I can certainly say without a doubt, this was the most scared I have ever been at any point in my life, before or since.

For the next fifteen minutes, neither of us said anything as the pilot wrestled with the controls. I was feeling sick because of the storm and was shaking with nervous energy.

We were constantly being thrown forwards, backwards, up, and down and from side to side. I had been on a few bumpy flights before where a sudden jerk of the plane had caused concern, but it had never been like this.

It was ten times worse! I thought, "If we don't crash it will be a miracle". The thoughts crossed my mind about the local newspaper headlines the next day, "Pilot and local business executives' aircraft is lost at sea".

The pilot broke our silence by saying, "I had better find out where we are". I naturally expected him to use the radio to find our location or some other piece of equipment. Instead, he reached down to his left side and pulled up a well-used wooden clipboard that had a map attached to it. A rusty old bull clip held this in place.

My mouth opened wide in complete horror as he let go of the steering apparatus, which made the engine slow down while the plane pointed itself in what I would describe as a slight dive. This was while we were still being thrown about violently. I was astonished as he opened the map and placed it over the entire windscreen.

I could not believe what I was seeing, as he spent some time trying to work out where we were on the chart.

He was attempting to point out places on the map, but could not do so with any accuracy because of the violent shaking and banging of the plane.

I wondered if we were going to fly into the water. This probably lasted for about a minute, but in all honesty, it seemed like hours. It was a complete and total nightmare!

After what seemed like an age, he folded the map up and put it back on the clipboard, putting it away on his side. Much to my relief. I realised I had been holding my breath through all the time that he looked at the map. He grabbed hold of the steering and pulled it towards him. The engine sped up as we climbed up again through the storm clouds.

We were still being violently shaken around continuously. I realised I had not let go of the frame of my seat since taking off.

I am sure that I embedded the shape of my fingers into the metal. We continued flying blindly in complete silence. The buffeting and shaking did not subdue in any way at all.

After about twenty further minutes, he did the same thing, shouting, "I need to check where we are again"! Just as before, he let go of the steering apparatus.

The engine slowed down, and the plane pointed itself at a slightly downward angle.

Once again, he reached down to his left side and pulled up the clipboard. Just as before, he opened the map and placed it over the entire windscreen. He still tried to point out places on the map, but he again could not, because of the constant buffeting and shaking of the aircraft.

Back in Swansea airport, the older man confirmed what Sue had told me the day before.

The flight would take approximately forty-five minutes. We had been flying for around an hour when he again let go of the steering and grabbed the clipboard for a third time.

"I will not let you do that again, I thought. He started to reach down for the clipboard and looked really startled as my years of martial arts experience came into play. I moved at speed and forcibly held his left arm down In a vice like grip, so that he could not move.

We wrestled for a few seconds as the plane engine slowed, with the aircraft once again going into a slight dive. I thrust out my right hand, grabbing hold of the clipboard. With a loud roar, "Yeeargh"! I ripped it right out of his hand.

As I pulled it away, I shouted loudly with an expression of crazed ferocity, screaming,

"LOOK MATE, I AM HOLDING THE MAP. YOU FLY THE *!!*!!* PLANE"! At that moment, I must have resembled a violent maniac.

We sat silently for a few seconds whilst still being thrown all over the place by the constant bashing of the wind on the plane. I must have looked quite frightening as I lent as far away as possible from the pilot, twisting to my right side, tightly folding my arms over my chest, completely hiding the clipboard from his sight. There was no way on earth that I would let him get hold of the map again.

I shouted forcefully, leaving a pause between the words to make sure he understood. "I AM HOLDING THE MAP. GOT-IT"!

Other than the noise of the wind battering against the aircraft, it was as if there was complete silence in those few seconds. He looked at my crazed expression and then stared down at my arms for a moment. I could see the realisation on his face that there was no way he was getting the map.

It was now mine. I had taken ownership of it. I would not surrender it in any way. He eventually submitted by saying, "Er.... OK, you hold on to it then", nodding his head in a reassuring manner.

I carefully opened the map and held it up so that he did not have to let go of the steering controls. Even though we were still being violently shaken and buffeted, he managed to look at it for a while and shouted, "We must be near the airport by now, but I can't see it because of the heavy cloud cover. I am going to make a circle around the area until we can find it!

The weather was still awful, plus I was also feeling quite air sick due to the violent turbulence,

but it encouraged me to learn that we were supposedly near the airport.

We could have easily blown by the winds to China for all I knew. We flew around in a circle for about ten minutes.

Eventually, after much staring, an opening appeared. Through a small gap in the clouds, I managed to see part of the airport, shouting, and pointing using exaggerated body language, "It's down there"! Thinking to myself, "Thank God for that".

He contacted the control tower, and we started our descent. It was just as terrifying as our take off had been. As we broke through the clouds, he continued to fight against the weather, trying to keep the wings as straight as possible. Finally, with a loud thud, we bounced along on the runway until he managed to slow the plane down and taxied over towards the main building.

He stopped outside of the passenger terminal and said, "Right Moray.

I am going back to Swansea now. I will return to pick you up at 4.30 pm". He put his thumb up and said, "Okay, I will see you later".

I was met by a colleague, and went to my meetings incredibly grateful to be alive. I shared the story with the entire group, who all laughed at my almost unbelievable journey,

Even though I was very busy throughout the day, I really hoped the weather would improve, but it didn't change in any way at all.

ALARMED...

Definition:

WORRIED OR FRIGHTENED

Synonyms:

DISTRESSED

DISMAYED

STARTLED

PERHAPS THE PILOT CRASHED INTO THE SEA?

Chapter Four – Waiting nervously

It delighted me that my meetings had gone very well. The sales teams had all agreed to be merged into my region. I was very excited about the prospects, and I was feeling really motivated.

I noticed that the windsock was blowing completely straight as I was dropped off at the airport.

I was concerned to discover that my pilot had not arrived as arranged at 4:15 pm.

I started to get genuinely worried when a further half an hour had passed. In the light of this, I walked around the airport to see if I could find someone who could help me. I had no luck with that.

Being a small airport, I quickly found myself at the observation level, which was situated directly underneath the control tower. I peered into the sky and waited there for quite a while, but there was still no sign of him.

After a few more minutes, I made the decision that there was no other option than to speak to someone who worked in the control tower.

To my surprise, just a few feet away from where I was standing, there was a door next to the observation level.

It was locked with a sign that was fixed to the door saying, **"CONTROL TOWER. AUTHORISED PERSONNEL ONLY"**.

I waited for a while to see if anyone would come along, but no one did. I needed to do something, and thought to myself, "There is nothing else for it". I banged hard on the door with the side of my fist in a hammer fashion a few times.

I had used this technique many times as a karateka, which meant that I struck the door with significant power. Boom! Boom! Boom! The sound of my karate strikes, known as a "Hammer fist", echoed around the passenger terminal, causing some waiting passengers to look up or jump.

Eventually the door was answered by a tall man who looked at me quizzically for a moment before saying, "Yes", in a quite irritated fashion.

I started to explain my predicament, but he wouldn't listen to me. Instead he interrupted me saying,

"You shouldn't be up here, it's out of bounds to people who are not authorised. Go back downstairs immediately". He was clearly very agitated by my actions.

He didn't want to listen to me. So I decided not to move until eventually, through my lack of motion, I finally got him to pay attention to me.

I explained that the aircraft I was waiting for was approaching an hour late. I gave a brief description of my flight to Exeter that morning and asked, "Is there any way that you could contact the pilot by radio? He was still quite irritated, but asked me, "What airport is he flying from"? "Swansea," I answered. " He stood there and thought about it for a moment and told me, "I will see what I can do". "Thank you, I really appreciate it", I replied.

He sent me downstairs and gave me another telling off, making me promise not to return, saying definitely, "Don't come up to the control tower again. I will come and find you". "Thanks again", I answered. He spun around, walked back in the direction of the control tower, taking treble steps up the stairs until I lost sight of him.

About 10 minutes later, he found me as promised, but had an overly concerned look on his face as he shared the news. He gestured that we move out of the earshot of waiting passengers leaning in towards me, decreasing the volume of his voice. "We have tried to contact the pilot by radio, to no avail. We have also been in contact with Swansea airport control, who told us he set off at around 3.30 pm. His arrival time was 4.15 pm". I looked at my watch.

It was now approaching 5.10 pm. "You will just have to wait", he finished. I thanked the man once again for his help and waited out on the observation deck. I felt quite alarmed.

The sky was just as dark as it had been that morning, and the wind was still as bad. I went back to the observation deck which was basically a platform that went around in a circle directly underneath the control tower. I was just wearing a business suit at the time and was freezing as I waited.

I stared into the distance, hoping upon hope to see the aircraft. After about five minutes or so, a small plane broke through the clouds. It was being blown from side to side while its wings were going up and down. As it came closer, I could see that it was my flight. "At last", I thought.

The Pilot obviously struggled to keep the wings straight until he touched down, bouncing, and wobbling along as he went.

He eventually taxied round to the area in front of the terminal building where I was waiting, because I had made my way outside and stood waving my arms until he saw me.

He taxied over and stopped the plane like he was doing an emergency stop on a driving test, turned off the engine, and opened his door. He virtually fell out of the cockpit as he clambered out.

He looked at me and said, "Hi, sorry I am late, I nearly didn't make it".

"Oh, that really is terrific news. Thanks again", I thought sarcastically.

GOBSMACKED...

Definition:

SO SURPRISED THAT YOU CANNOT SPEAK

Synonyms:

DUMBFOUNDED

FLABBERGASTED

DUMBSTRUCK

I WAS COMPLETELY GOBSMACKED!

Chapter Five – Will I ever get home?

On hearing him say that he nearly didn't make it. I was totally gobsmacked. I stood there for a moment in complete silence. My thoughts of sarcasm quickly turned to feelings of dread. I looked at the plane and said to myself, "Oh no, I've got to fly back in that thing again, and In this weather. Not again". At that moment, I thought to myself, "We are doomed".

My eyes then turned to the pilot, who resembled someone that was a little seasick. I asked him,

"Are you sure that you are OK mate"? because he also looked as white as a sheet. "I'm fine, thanks," he replied. He looked at me, and enthusiastically rubbed his hands together and said with a cheerful grin, "Right, come on then. I have got to get you back to Swansea".

I don't know if it is even possible. But in those few seconds, I was even more gobsmacked than before. It was unbelievable.

I just stood there looking at him in silence, wondering if this was actually a nightmare. Would I wake up soon? "Come on then. We have to get a move on," he said urgently. He motioned for me to climb into the cockpit.

Just as I had done in Swansea, I put on my life jacket and tied the cords. It was yet another reminder of what lay ahead.

How I got back into the plane I will never know. I had been really scared on the first flight. Now I was really terrified. The dictionary, give a good explanation to describe how I was feeling, "Terrified beyond human comprehension".

We then went through the same process as before. The pilot checked with the control tower that we were OK for take-off. The voice in my headphones gave us the all clear. Another bumpy taxi ride along the runway followed this. Once again, we had a horrific take-off, which was remarkably similar to the one I had experienced at Swansea. I suppose I was getting used to it by this time.

Thankfully, there was no rain to greet us as we climbed through the air, but we were still being buffeted and thrown about as before.

We continued to climb until we eventually reached the dark clouds, which must have been quite low, because we were soon flying above them.

As we broke through, we flew into bright sunshine, which was a great welcome. The short flight home was still quite bumpy, because we had powerful winds behind us.

It honestly felt as if we were flying in a ballistic missile because I could tell that we were moving at great speed. The powerful winds were pushing us along at quite a rate.

In what seemed no time at all, we could see the Swansea coast because the clouds had virtually disappeared ahead of us. It was still very windy in the area, but we had a good landing and even felt good enough to chat as we taxied back to the Air Aid hut.

On our arrival, the pilot turned off the engine. We had a brief chat and laughed about the day we had together. We also talked about the amusing 'Map incident'.

I was very glad to be alive. I apologised sincerely for my actions regarding the map. Explaining how I was alarmed by his opening off the map on the windscreen.

The splendid news was that I arrived at my evening recruitment seminar with time to spare.

The event went very well, with a number of candidates progressing to the final interview stage of our interview process.

Remarkably, the day had turned out to be a very successful one. I went home and had an early night. I slept like a log.

I have flown frequently since that time, on much larger planes. Very often, I will look out of the window as we take off. I wait until we reach a certain height and say to myself. "Dead now".

Other titles you can read by

Moray LWH McGuffie

A Fall

From The Top

Climbing high up the ladder of success in martial arts, then in the world of business, only to fall from the top

My Story
Moray LWH McGuffie

Moray was born into a showbiz family. To those outside, everything seemed fine. The truth was that his home was a drunken and violent one. The split up of his parent's marriage and other events made him a worrier. Aged fifteen, he discovered the martial art of Karate in which he excelled, building his confidence and self-belief. He reached high ranking black belt grades to become a professional instructor. Unfortunately, an injury stopped this suddenly.

Moving into financial services he used the disciplines he had learned from karate to climb the corporate ladder, becoming known as "Quantum Leap". Success brought the lifestyle that people dream of. Reaching the peak of success, problems occurred which caused him to literally fall from the top.

This failure caused him to feel despair and left him contemplating suicide. A chance meeting with two young businesspeople led to events that changed the direction of his life. Discover what it feels like to be a highflyer, quickly followed by a rapid fall to the bottom.

★★★★★   His story is amazing and a real page turner.

★★★★★   Falling from great heights isn't always a bad thing.

★★★★★   A truly amazing and inspiring journey.

★★★★★   I Could not put it down.

Available at Amazon, on Kindle and from any good book store

Coming Soon

Real Job Interview

Secrets

How to succeed where others fail

A recruitment professional provides you
with an effective range of strategies that
work through proven results

Learn how you can gain the edge over
other candidates in the job interview process

Moray LWH McGuffie

Job interviews are often the cause of considerable anxiety and stress for people who apply for jobs. This book will provide you with easy to understand techniques and strategies that work through proven results in the interview process. Importantly, they can help to give you the edge over other candidates who have also applied.

The areas covered are explained in language that is simple to follow. You will learn many of the errors that candidates make in the interview process, as well as how you can send positive signals to the interviewer to create higher levels of rapport, thereby increasing your likeability factor.

Discover the real secrets of succeeding where others fail:

- The importance of preparation
- Interviewer types
- Understanding the communication process
- Arriving for the interview
- Interview behaviour
- Stress and anxiety busters
- Typical job interview questions and answers
- How to respond to the offer of an interview
- Body language, including photo examples
- What to do if you are not offered a job
- Why you may need to change your approach
- Examples of questions you should ask
- Plus much more

Moray is a highly experienced recruiter and team builder, having worked in the UK as well as internationally. In recent years he has spent much of his time t eaching and training people on all aspects of the interview process.

ISBN: 9798478887230

'Absolutely Terrified'

ISBN: 9798478887230

'Absolutely Terrified'

Copyright © 2021

ISBN: 9798478887230

'Absolutely Terrified

ISBN: 9798478887230

'Absolutely Terrified'

'Absolutely Terrified'

ISBN: 9798478887230

'Absolutely Terrified'

Copyright © 2021

ISBN: 9798478887230

'Absolutely Terrified'

Copyright © 2021

ISBN: 9798478887230

'Absolutely Terrified'

ISBN: 9798478887230

'Absolutely Terrified'

Copyright © 2021

ISBN: 9798478887230

'Absolutely Terrified'

ISBN: 9798478887230

'Absolutely Terrified'

ISBN: 9798478887230

'Absolutely Terrified'

ISBN: 9798478887230

'Absolutely Terrified'

Printed in Great Britain
by Amazon